Toys in Space

Some other books by Mini Grey

Traction Man Is Here!
Traction Man Meets Turbo Dog
Traction Man and the Beach Odyssey
Three by the Sea
The Adventures of the Dish and the Spoon
Egg Drop
Ginger Bear
The Very Smart Pea and the Princess-to-Be

For Janet Schulman

E
420-9055

THIS IS A BORZOI BOOK PUBLISHED BY ALFRED A. KNOPF

Copyright © 2012 by Mini Grey

All rights reserved. Published in the United States by Alfred A. Knopf, an imprint
of Random House Children's Books, a division of Random House, Inc., New York.
Originally published in Great Britain by Jonathan Cape, an imprint of Random House
Children's Books, a division of the Random House Group Ltd., London, in 2012.

Knopf, Borzoi Books, and the colophon are registered trademarks
of Random House, Inc.

Visit us on the Web! randomhouse.com/kids

Educators and librarians, for a variety of teaching tools,
visit us at RHTeachersLibrarians.com

Library of Congress Cataloging-in-Publication Data is available upon request.

ISBN 978-0-307-97812-7 (trade) — ISBN 978-0-307-97815-8 (lib. bdg.)

MANUFACTURED IN CHINA
May 2013
10 9 8 7 6 5 4 3 2 1

First American Edition

Toys in Space

MINI GREY

Alfred A. Knopf
NEW YORK

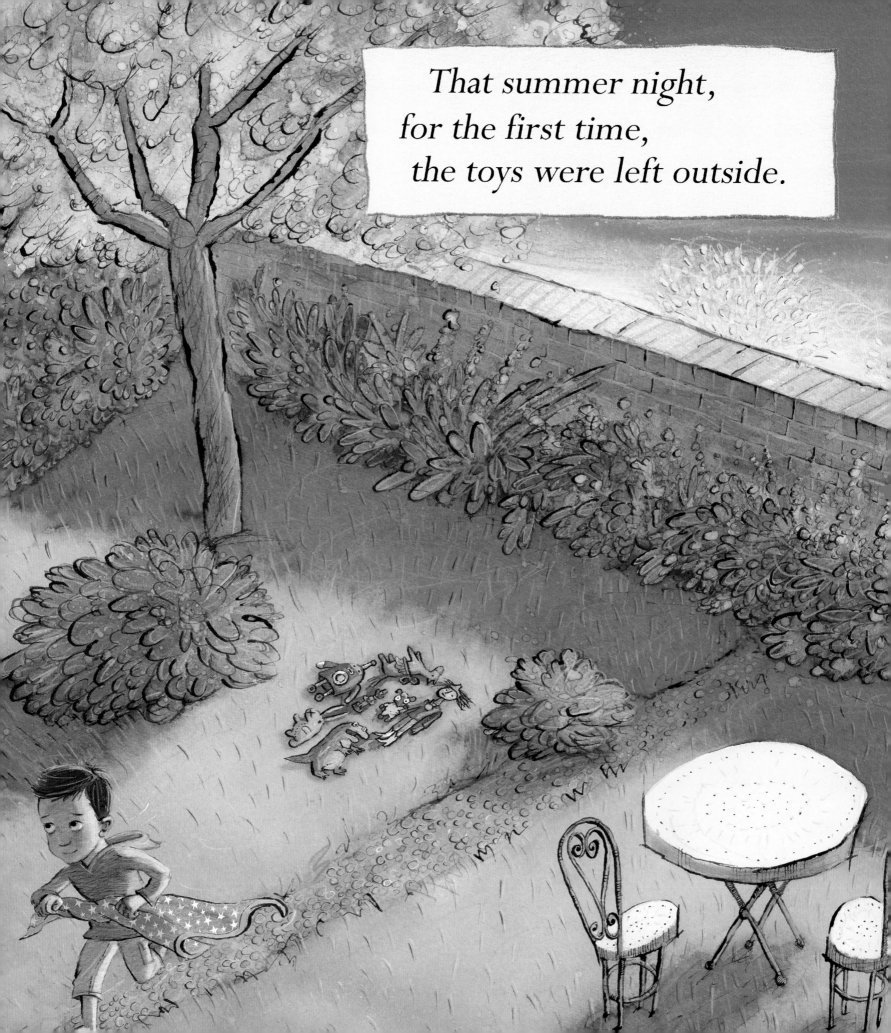

That summer night,
for the first time,
the toys were left outside.

The sun went down,

the sky grew dark,

and, for the very first time…

Everyone was quiet
for a while.

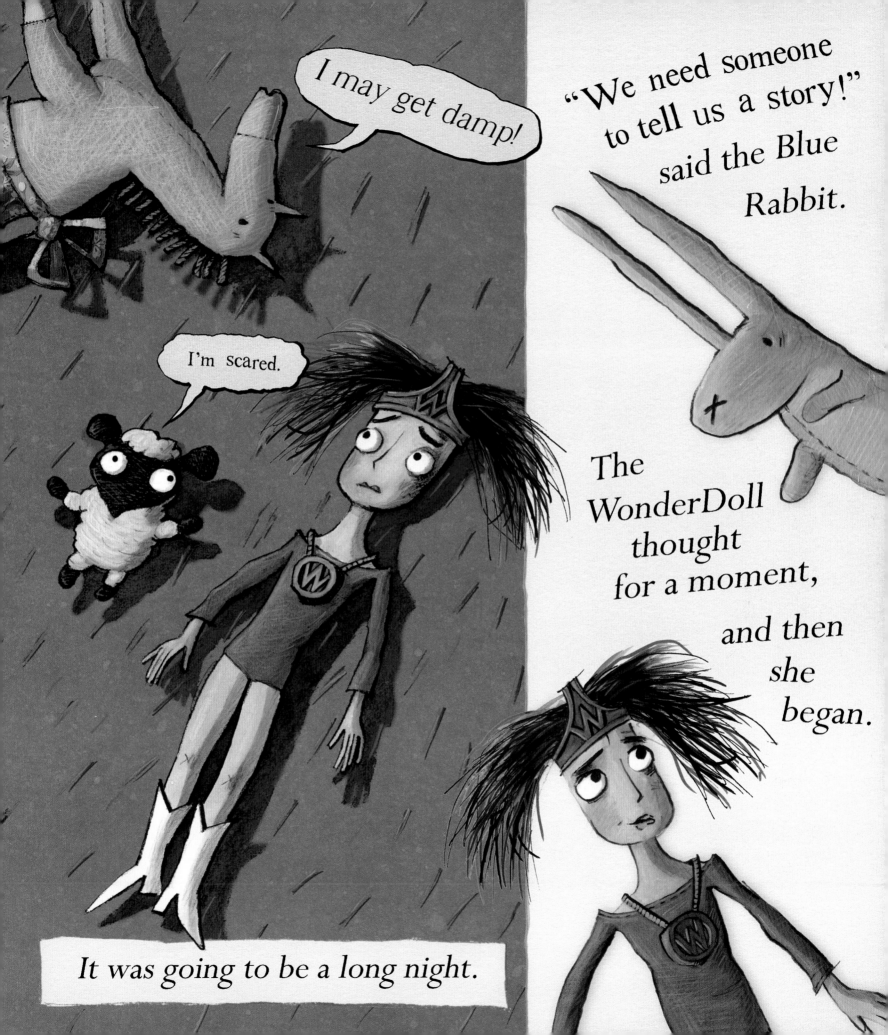

Once upon a time *(the WonderDoll said)*, there were seven toys left out in the garden:

a resourceful Pink Horse,

a brave Small Sheep,

a clever Blue Rabbit,

a strong little Cowboy,

a thoughtful green Dinosaur,

a helpful windup Robot,

and a WonderDoll.

Well, the sun went down and the toys saw the stars for the very first time.

And then one of the stars started to grow. It got bigger and bigger and bigger.

And the toys realized it
was actually not a star at all—
it was a spaceship!

And the spaceship
opened up a bright
hole and
beamed
the toys
up into it.

Well *(went on the WonderDoll)*, the toys were inside the spaceship and feeling a bit worried, as you can imagine.

Then a door opened...

Someone might get their stuffing probed!

...and the toys saw a shadow in the doorway.

I don't think anyone's stuffing *should* be probed!

Oh dear, there might be an accident!

No dang drooling alien is probing me!

In came a space creature.

What did it look like?

Was it drooling?

It looked rather like a glove
and it was wearing pajamas
and its eyes were red
from crying.

What was it called?

We will call it the
Hoctopize for now.

The Hoctopize looked carefully at the toys.
But none was the toy it was searching for.

The Hoctopize showed the toys
a picture of its Cuddles, who was
lost.

Then they parachuted all the Lost Toys down toward Earth.

The toys helped the Hoctopize to realize that all those Thousand Lost Toys had to be returned to their real homes.

But how do they know where to send them?

Luckily, the Hoctopize was very organized and had labeled them all with their addresses.

It put a stamp on each label to help with the delivery.

ar the Pond
2 Rockery Prospect
Puddlington

Picnic Table
Front Lawn
37 Spoon Drift
West Cutlery

Once they had gone, the Hoctopize sat down and cried. It still didn't have its Cuddles.

The toys need to make it feel better!

Then the Dinosaur had an idea—they could have a party to cheer up the Hoctopize.

Everyone had jobs to do:
Blue Rabbit and Pink Horse made a cake,
WonderDoll and Small Sheep made party hats, and
Robot and Dinosaur did the decorations.

And what about the Cowboy? What did the Cowboy do?

The Cowboy organized all the games.

zp!

Hey! You! Stop! You're out!

They played musical chairs and musical statues.

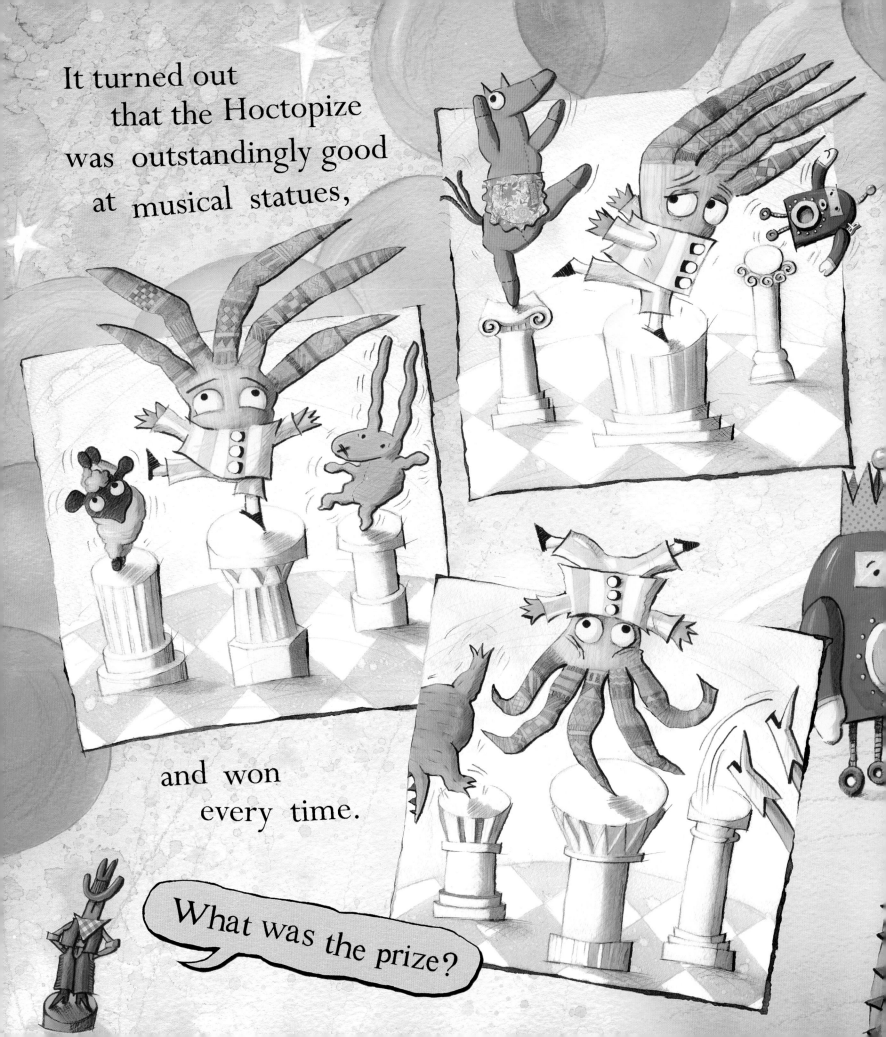

It turned out
that the Hoctopize
was outstandingly good
at musical statues,

and won
every time.

What was the prize?

They gave it the WonderDoll's medal as the prize.

But the toys can't stay in space forever!

THEY NEED TO GO HOME!

Someone will be missing them!

Our toys have to return
(the WonderDoll carried on).
They each hold a balloon to drift down,
and everybody takes a piece of cake.

The Hoctopize waves goodbye.

And down down down

through dark space

and into blue sky

and through clouds

and toward the ground

float the toys.

The WonderDoll stopped.

The toys opened
their eyes—the dawn
had happened.

It was a new day,
and soon they would
be found.

Oh yes (said the WonderDoll),
of course it will find its Cuddles.

It will be
in the last
place it looks.

Things
always are.